Diary of Steve the Noob

Steve the Noob

Thank You

Thank you for picking up a copy of my book. I spent many hours putting this book together, so I hope that you will enjoy reading it. I always try to make the story as interesting as possible and to add a little bit of humor here and there; I just hope that you get my jokes.

As a Minecraft player, it brings me great joy to be able to share my stories with you. The game is fun and entertaining, and surprisingly, writing about it can be almost just as fun. Once you are done reading this book, if you enjoyed it, please take a moment to leave a review. It will help other people discover this book. If after reading it, you realize that you hate it with such passion, please feel free to leave me a review anyway. I enjoy reading what people think about my books and writing style. I hope that a lot of people will like this book and encourage me to keep writing. Thanks in advance.

Special thanks to readers of my previous books. Thank you for taking the time to leave a review. I appreciate it so much; your support means so much to me. I will continue to keep writing and will try to provide the highest quality of unofficial Minecraft books. Thank you for your support.

Monday

I woke up in a strange land as flat as flat can be with no mountains for miles on out. There was not a single soul around me. I was alone, all by myself. Actually, I wasn't completely alone, there were some green looking boxes hopping around in the distance. Next to me was a treasure box left out in the open. I immediately cracked that thing having never backed down from a freebie. Inside, I found tons of useful stuff like a wooden sword and an axe.

I decided to approach a green looking thing to ask for directions, but when it noticed me, it started hopping faster and faster towards me. Upon closer inspection, I thought this creature looked like green jelly dessert; it was actually kind of cute. But next thing I knew, that stupid cube jelly thing was jumping on top of me, smashing my delicate organs.

"AHHH! Please stop! I just ate too much and now you're squishing me!" I yelled as it slimed me with green goo.

There was no response from the green menace; it just continued hammering me into the ground.

I couldn't take it anymore, so I pulled out my flimsy wooden sword. "Fine, if that's the way you want it, you're due for a whooping," I said bravely.

I swung and I swung, full of misses and close calls; I hardly hurt the thing and I was already bleeding out and down to a third of my life. It was time to run. I zigged and I zagged and darted in tons of different directions hoping that I would lose him, but surprisingly for a box with bad aerodynamics, he was darn fast and was on me like green on grass. Off in the distance, I could see a small village. I thought surely someone there could help me.

I ran and I ran, limping and groaning, but I finally made it to the village. I found many villagers there, but they just looked at me with blank stares. They had dull eyes and big o' noses. They were quite reminiscent of a particular squid I once knew; he lived next to a pineapple.

"Help me, please! That box monster is trying to kill me!" I begged them.

Hmmmrph…

Hmaaarph…

That was all I heard from them. They continued about their business as the angry green box wailed on me, crushing me like an ant. What hurt the most was that they didn't even bother to watch me get whooped.

I tried one last desperate attempt to lose the green threat. I ran in circles and hid behind a corner until at last, I finally lost him and he forgot about me. I fell to the floor, exhausted.

At that point, a villager approached me. "Hi, sorry we couldn't help you out earlier. We have a deal with the green boxes; they don't hurt us, and we don't hurt them. I guess they just don't like you."

"Oh," I replied, bleeding everywhere. "Can you help me now?"

"Sure. Here, have some carrots and potatoes."

I was like, "Really?" I just got my butt kicked and now you're giving me potatoes? But surprisingly, when I consumed the carrots and potatoes, it quickly restored some energy. Then I explained to him my situation.

"I woke up today and here I am. I don't remember who I am or where I came from."

"I see. Well, you can rest here until you recover your health and memory," said the villager. Then he introduced himself as Joe the librarian.

I was feeling stronger now. "Thanks, Joe," I said while getting up.

"Come on, stranger. Let's get you inside. Darkness is coming."

"*Darkness is coming?*" I asked. "What's so scary about darkness?"

"Once the night is upon us, these lands will be crawling with evil, mean creatures. It is best we don't stick around and greet them. By the way, what should I call you?"

"My name? I don't remember it. I don't remember anything," I told him.

"Well, okay. Let's just call you Steve, Steve the noob."

I was hesitant about the noob part, but whatever, I was stuck in a strange, new land with nothing but the clothes on my back. We arrived at the library and sealed up the door tight. Within a few hours, the peaceful little village had become a nightmare. It was filled with creepy crawlers of all sizes. There were zombies, spiders, and skeleton warriors all knocking at our door. We remained as quiet as possible, but I could hear them breathing through the walls. The monsters moaned, groaned, and wandered all over. It was then that I realized that this village was in trouble, and somebody needed to do something about it.

Tuesday

As the Sun rose, there was a sigh of relief from the villagers. I learned that these night crawlers could not stand the sun. They would burst on fire like fireworks on the 4th of July. Well, that was only some of them. A few of the creatures remained and we had to clear them out. We worked together and drove the remaining monsters out of the village.

I met the village chief later in the day.

"Welcome to our humble village, Steve. Stay as long as you need to," said the chief. "We will share our food supply and shelter with you."

"Thank you, sir. It is very much appreciated. How can I ever repay you?" I asked.

"I'm sure you will think of something," he replied with a smile, and then walked away.

Later that day, I did think of something. I thought that if we had some sort of wall, maybe we could protect the village from these nightly invasions. So, Joe and I set out to build a wall made of dirt. Why dirt? Because it was simply the most abundant source of material at the time. We were working all afternoon and late into the evening. Before we knew it, night was upon us again and the creatures were already here.

Joe and I ran as fast as we could to find shelter from the night. As we were running, Joe tripped and sprained his ankle. The zombies saw that and homed in on us.

"Leave me, Steve! You won't make it if you carry me," he yelled.

"No, never leave a man behind! I got you, buddy," I replied as I threw him over my shoulder.

At this point, the zombies were really close and the skeleton archers were sending hails of arrows our way. I ran towards the closest building I saw, and at the time I remembered wishing that Joe wasn't so fat. Arrows were whizzing by, zombies were close behind, and me, I was struggling to carry my only buddy. Against the odds, we made it to the building, and to my surprised, I made there without a scratch.

All those arrows and not a single one touched me. Man, I'm super lucky, I thought to myself.

Then... I noticed Joe's back. He had like, 50 arrows stuck in his back. He was already long gone before we made it to safety.

"Noooo!! Why?!" I cried. "WHY?!?"

There was another person in the building.

"It was his time. Let him go," said the stranger.

The stranger turned out to be the village's cleric. He knew a lost cause when he saw one.

"The best you can do now is avenge him," the cleric said.

"Avenge him, I shall!" I screamed and raced to the rooftop.

The building we ran to happened to be the tallest building in the village. On the rooftop, you can see pretty much everything. There, I saw each and every creature trespassing in our little village. And there, I swore I would get my revenge for Joe.

Wednesday

I have decided to become the defender of this small village. I will become its champion and protector. There will be no more casualties on my watch. The first thing I did today was set out to create a bow and some arrows. I knew that from the rooftop I could be like a sniper and pick off my targets with ease. But to create a bow and some arrows, I first needed a crafting table first. Fortunately, this was simple enough to make.

While gathering materials for the table and bow, the green box returned to troll me. But this time, I was prepared for battle. I knew what was coming, and I wanted it to come.

I pulled out my cheap wooden sword and whacked it furiously at the box.

It staggered him for a moment.

So, I took the opportunity and whacked him again and again.

But out of nowhere, his friends came and backed him up. Suddenly, it was 3 against 1.

It didn't matter, I was ready for battle.

Actually, it did matter, 3 vs 1 proved a bit too much. They worked together, bouncing one after the next, and they got me down to a quarter of my life.

I ducked behind a building and ate some carrots, potatoes, and apples, hoping for a quick energy boost, so that I could keep fighting.

The rush of sugar and carbs kicked in, and I suddenly had the strength to fight on.

I figured out their timing and attack pattern. If only I had a long wooden spear like the Spartans of old, I would be able to easily keep these boxes at bay.

But alas, I am stuck with this short wooden sword; forced to go close range. If I am lucky, I might be able to get a special move in: *Splinter Strike*, which causes damage over time. Aw, yeah, but that is if I am lucky.

The fight continues for the next half hour. I didn't expect the fight to last this long, but those darn boxes are able to self-replicate or something. I whack one down and three more takes its place.

Finally, I finished the last of them. No more boxes. Victory was mine.

I continued to gather materials.

I returned to the village to build the crafting table. I was surprised to see some of the villagers had taken upon themselves to try to complete the wall that Joe and I had started. It was a touching effort.

I made a bow and some arrows, another wooden sword, a pickaxe, and some other tools.

Later that night, high up upon the rooftop I made my stand. Arrow upon arrow I let loose upon those zombies. I showered them with vengeance and laughed maniacally throughout the night.

"Taste my fury, you brain leeches!" I yelled.

The zombies moaned and the spiders screeched.

"Eat arrows all night, soul suckers!" I provoked.

Then…I ran out of arrows…

There was a mob of angry monsters below me, and I had nothing to offer them. I couldn't hurt them anymore, and they wanted me so bad.

So, I did the next best thing. I pulled out my pickaxe and chipped away at the stone walls of our high tower. I took the bits and pieces of stone and hurled them over the edge.

Needless to say, I shut up those monsters good that night.

Thursday

I woke up the next morning to a loud ruckus. The whole village was cheering for me. Everyone heard about what I did last night and commended my bravery. The chief met me later in the day and gave me a medal for my service.

"Steve, thank you for defending our dear village. You are exactly what we need," said the chief.

"It is nothing, sir. I did what I had to do, but my work is far from over," I replied.

The chief seemed impressed. "Good," he said, "we need more people like you. Please, help yourself to our crops. We need our hero big and strong."

I thanked the chief and headed off. There was much work to be done; it wasn't the time to celebrate. I needed to come up with, like, a thousand more arrows.

How am I ever going to obtain that many arrows? I thought to myself.

A few moments later, a villager named Jack approached me.

"I saw you last night, raining arrows from the night sky; it was a beautiful thing to watch," Jack told me. "But if you want to continue spraying arrows like bullets from a machine gun, you'll need something called an infinity book."

That last part peaked my curiosity. "*Infinity book*? What is that?" I asked.

The villager said, "It is a magical enchantment book that will allow you to fire your bow endlessly."

I got super excited at that point because that book was the answer to my problem. "Where can I find such a book? Please tell me!" I pleaded.

Jack smirked. "Oh, I have one right here! But you can't have it," he responded.

"What?! Why not? It would be so useful in defending the village."

"Ah, yes, but I like being able to deny you of something that you *really* want."

"But—"

He walked away.

That day I made my first enemy. Later, I found out from the other villagers that Jack was known as Jack the jerk. It all made sense.

Whatever.

I was annoyed and disappointed by Jack. I decided to just make my own arrows for the time being, and for that, I needed more wood. Unfortunately, I couldn't find a single tree nearby.

Later in the day, I found out where Jack lived. When he was not looking, I took an axe to the back of his house. I figured since he wouldn't help me get unlimited arrows from the enchanted book, I'd just use his house to craft some arrows instead; seems fair enough. I chopped and I chopped until my inventory was full of wood, then I took off running before anyone saw me.

I returned to my crafting table and made some arrows. I also figured that I should get some armor just in case I have to get up close and personal with these baddies. So, I set out to search for cows and horses to slay.

I found a bunch of cows hanging out near the outskirts of the village. I whacked them a few times; they just took the beating and fell over.

Easy peasy, I thought.

I started skinning them for their leather hide. It was a messy job, and I felt guilty slaying those innocent cows, but it had to be done. I needed to protect my silky soft skin and delicate features from zombie bites and arrows from skeleton archers.

I went back to the village and crafted my first set of leather armor. I only had enough to make a leather tunic, but it was good enough. The sun was starting to set, so that meant it was time to go get ready for the night.

I felt confident because I had new protective gear and more arrows. I climbed the ladder to the rooftop and stood at my post. I watched as the moon slowly rose and the night started to echo with sounds of monstrous creatures.

With my trusty bow in hand and arrows at the ready, I let it rain.

Friday

The next morning, I woke up on the rooftop. The villagers were cheering again.

"Another safe night gone by!" they cheered. "All hail, Steve the hero!"

I was a bit embarrassed. "Thank you, my fellow villagers," I said. "We have defended our village for yet another night. Today, let us double our efforts and complete the wall, so that we may all sleep soundly at night."

Everyone agreed. We got out our shovels, and we continued to build the wall made of dirt around our village. It was a daunting task. Though the village was not that big, there was still a lot of ground to cover.

I wish we had some kind of sturdier material to use for this wall, I thought to myself. Dirt, well, just looks cheap, not only that, it is weak and um, dirty. Oh well, I guess beggars can't be choosers. We will just have to make do with what we've got.

Besides building the wall, I also took this opportunity to rebuild the high tower that I've made my post. The tower was badly damaged from all my digging on Wednesday night. I didn't have stone to use to repair the tower, so I had to use dirt again. The tower was no longer magnificent looking or pretty, but it would work just fine.

We were about half way done building the wall before night fell. As usual, I went up to the tower to man my post. The villagers all ran home and locked their doors.

In the distance, I spotted a villager running towards the village. He was being chased by the emerging zombies. I knew he wasn't going to make it to safety if I didn't help him. So, I ditched my tower and grabbed my wooden sword and ran out to escort the villager.

I ran to him. "Come with me if you want to live!" I yelled.

"Okay! I'm right behind you," he replied.

There were monsters popping out at every corner.

"Ahhhh! Help me!" he screamed as zombies grabbed his shirt.

I drew out my wooden sword and swung it with all my might.

TWHACK! TWHACK!

The zombies let him go, but they were interested in me now.

"Rrrraaaggghh!" was all I heard as I swung my cheap sword at them. I was doing fine holding them off at first, but more and more zombies came. Before I knew it, they were chasing me down like a train.

I decided to change my fighting strategy to something I knew always worked. I activated my circle strafing technique to combat the train of zombies. The circle strafing technique allowed me to keep a small footprint, while maximizing damage output and reducing damage input through dodging. It worked like a charm. It wasn't long before a dozen zombies laid at my feet.

After I cleared the path of zombies, we made way to the tower. There, I learned the villager I had just saved was named Marco.

"Thank you for saving me, dear hero," he said. "I am forever in your debt. What can I do to repay you?"

I told him, "Help me fight this invasion by crafting me more arrows."

He agreed.

Throughout the night, I would shoot non-stop while Marco constructed more arrows for me. We made a pretty good team that night.

Saturday

The next morning everyone got to work on the wall right away. The villagers were excited about completing the wall because then, they would be able to stay out late at night instead of hiding indoors. It seemed like a pretty cool concept to be able to stay out late and not have to fear for your life.

We finished the wall around 3 P.M., and it was time to celebrate. The butchers brought out their best meats, the farmers brought out their best produce, and the armorers brought out their best gears to show off. It was a fun and joyful time. Everyone was happy and at ease.

Some of the villagers were excellent cooks. They made baked potatoes, cakes, rabbit stews and steaks. It was all so delicious, and I totally pigged out. I was being a little fatty, but I didn't care. We deserved it. We had earned it after all that digging and building. I ate to my heart's content and took the rest of the night off. I had finally earned my rest.

Not before long, night came upon us. We were all standing outside, and we heard the noises of the monsters increase little by little. Everyone was anxious and worried. From atop my tower, I could see the horde of monsters outside our newly built wall.

They tried to get through, but I guess the dirt was thick enough to hold them off. Everyone was relieved that the monsters couldn't break through, so we all continued to party throughout the night. As the hours went on, we became more and more confident in our wall; our plan had worked.

Unfortunately, we partied way into the night, and we got louder and louder. The noises we made drove the monsters into a frenzy. They were desperately clawing their way into the wall. Eventually, some of the zombies used the green cube monsters as a stepping staircase and climbed over the wall.

With more and more monsters climbing and standing on the wall, the wall shifted all over the place until finally it collapsed. Whose idea was it to build a wall out of dirt?! I tried to warn the villagers from atop of my tower, but it was already too late.

Instead of monsters approaching one by one slowly, now there was a sudden surge of 100s of monsters all at once. I couldn't hold them back. There were too many.

The villagers panicked and ran around in circles like dogs chasing their tails. In their panicked state, some of them forgot to lock their doors, and the zombies entered their homes.

From my tower, I heard were screams of terror; they were dying. But I couldn't help them, I was too busy trying to thin out the oncoming horde. Some brave villagers rushed out to try to save their dying neighbors, but alas, they also met the same fate.

As I was shooting arrows like a madman, a spider climbed a nearby building and jumped over to where I was standing; it bit me in the back. The sneaky back attack caused critical damage, and I was knocked back. Regrettably, I was standing on the tippy top of the roof, and I fell all the way down to the ground.

I hit my head hard and was knocked unconscious until the next morning…

Sunday

I awoke the next morning to the smell of burning zombie flesh and burnt wood. After the skeletons and zombies died out, I went to go look around. Some of the buildings were on fire, but I couldn't find any water to use to put it out. I did the next best thing by trying to spit on it; that didn't work. I thought about peeing on the building, but I didn't want to risk a ticket for public urination. So, I gave up, walked away and let the fire do its thing.

I continued looking around and found no one. There was not a sound to be heard, not a "hmmmrph" or a "haamph" around. There was not a soul in sight.

What happened last night? Where is everyone? I thought to myself.

I wandered the village for a while more, and then I found them; my heart sank. A dozen lifeless bodies of my former friends all huddled up in the library. It looked like the zombies and monsters trapped them, and they had nowhere to run.

I thought to myself, *Those fools! Why didn't they put in a rear exit? That's fire safety 101!*

Regardless, I had failed them. I was their defender; I was supposed to protect them, but here I am, the last survivor of this small village.

I don't know why only I survived; perhaps, I was meant for something more. But my shame was too great; I couldn't take it. I couldn't bear to stay in the ghost village any longer. So, I packed my things and headed off to whichever way the wind was blowing.

Knowing that I had failed in my mission greatly, I set off to make amends.

Who knows what I'll find if I keep walking in this direction? I thought to myself. *But whatever happens, I'm going to make up for letting my fellow villagers die. I will find a way to stop this nightly plague. I'll do whatever it takes, even if it kills me. That is my promise.*

Hero ending song plays

Can You Help Me Out?

Thanks for reading all the way through. I hope that you were truly entertained with the story and jokes. As a new writer, it is hard to get started; it is difficult to find an audience that wants to read my books. There are millions of books out there and sometimes it is super hard to find one specific book. But that's where you come in! You can help other readers find my books by leaving a simple review. It doesn't have to be a lengthy or well written review; it just has to be a few words and then click on the stars. It would take less than 5 minutes.

Seriously, that would help me so much, you don't even know. Every time I get a review, good or bad, it just fills me with motivation to keep on writing. It is a great feeling to know that somewhere out there, there are people who actually enjoy reading my books. Anyway, I would super appreciate it, thanks.

If you see new books from me in the future, you'll know that I wrote them because of your help. Thank you for supporting my work.

Special thanks again to previous readers and reviewers. Thank you for encouraging me to keep writing. I'll do my best to provide high quality books for you all.

My Other Books

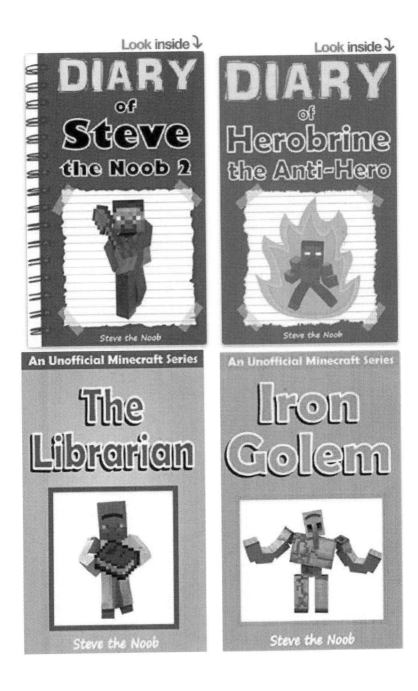

More Books

My Awesome List of Favorite Readers and Reviewers

My Awesome List of Favorite
Readers and Reviewers

W. shi "Jenn"

K.K "mysweetdees"

Mikail

WarCenturion

Stephanie Linn

Thank you so much for your support. You guys and girls rock!!

Jewel Shine

Minoscreeperslayer

RainbowCreeper

Sang Chul Choi

Misahti

Panisara W.

Astro Cat

AthanEnder

betsy

akaherobrine

James

Xaxier Edwards

leann xiao

Awesomeguy27

IsaBear556

Emma Hogan

Brandon Kim

Venu Gopal

Kathy

Yuan Cui

Sreekant Gottimukkala

Emma

Kayla Dingo

ZombieCupcake

Ding Zhou

Alex

spark527

Gator

Nick

devlin

Grant

MeowLord

Ducky MooMoo

Minecarft Book Girl

Jax/Blaze7381

Steve

Toni

Jane

Jacob

PigMaster4000

Skyler

Kayla Ding

Kareem

shard

Cole

TheGolem64

joshiewoshie12

Rosi

jhkim

Catboy327

Flamenarrow

MinerAwesomeGuy

Tommy

Teslageek

Calvin

Sid

J. Lada

Jason Hollister

TruReader

NinjaBoy899

Onjl

owlfeatherr

Dude89

Zachary Ln

haminal77

No One In Particular

Kate B.

Lynn Sims

Da Lover of Da Cats

love it

Michael Sonn

M. Hooper

dayli ward

cameron

J. Ely

john

shadow

matthkol

SkyMinecraft

Wendy

BobTheCow8274/Waylon

MarlaR

boi15

HappyPierceP

W

vighnesh

xNoobEvilBanana

TheJediMaster28

Lawton E. Paddock

JumpSlime

Ronan Bruno

Rainbow Cat 7562

Yan Guo

diamond girl

SkylarHearts

Joowon hwang

Dirt

Lucifer Hunt

Austyn

#1sonicfan

MineFox

Louis

JenaLuv & Boogie

nerf boy

kall20

Power

S.U.P.E.R. X.P.E.R. - -

TheRealLukester

yong ye

Cfee

PlasmaGamerYT/InvolateMoss22

LittleCrafter11

Nickelworld123

Snakebeast7865

Lora Bean

m78

Paul 14689

Alpha44

Xeevee

crazy creeper

TrollerDude34511

SurvivalMaster64

king of the cats

cake_girl

Shaojing Li

Snakebeast7865

Jazzgirl the defender

CC

Arcade gamer

Beth Worner

werewolfwes

furious_knight25

Ycrafter

Sam

AlabasterFoil32

Nexon1

ExplodingEmerald

joowon/superxper178

MJC

coolshinwon07

Xx_Gameknight_xX~ Conor

Charles Wen

LegoWarrior70

Foxfire

Thane

dm

Coolman100

CommanderBiffle

Reagan

Jairo

VinMannie the Gamer

matthkol

Hong Tian

YH

Stacey P.

Mona Maven

//the uber minecrafter//

Fire '¬'

FlipFlickerFlop3

Hamma

quantum_christopher128

r2d2

furious_knight25

Modded_Gamers

EmeraldGolem

Christo and Jon

adorkable cow

Ruffarian01

ExplodingEmerald